The Queen's Spaghetti

Patricia Cleveland-Peck
Illustrated by Tim Archbold

HarperCollins *Children's Books*

Queen Nellie was a big happy queen. She lived with her husband King Jim in an untidy castle on the edge of town. They hadn't got much money but they had a large garden, a small field, a wood with nine trees and a great many animals.

One evening, Queen Nellie came indoors and said, "What shall I cook for supper tonight?" She had been working in the garden all day and she was very hungry.

"I know," she said to herself, "I'll make spaghetti with a tomato sauce. King Jim does enjoy that."

King Jim was very good at sharing all the cooking and castlework but Queen Nellie liked to get him a meal when he'd been out at work all day. To make some money King Jim worked part time at the Royal Mint.

Queen Nellie put some water on to boil in a large pan. Because she was so hungry she put in lots and lots and lots of spaghetti.

Then she began the sauce. She sang a little song as she worked. She chopped onions and tomatoes and garlic and fried them until they sizzled and fizzled, filling the kitchen with a lovely smell.

But as the spaghetti cooked, it began to swell up.
Soon the big saucepan was overflowing.

"Oh dear," said the queen and she ran and fetched
another saucepan. She put half the spaghetti into
it. But still the spaghetti kept swelling up and soon
both saucepans were overflowing.

"Oh dear, oh dear," said Queen Nellie and she ran and fetched two more saucepans. She put some spaghetti into each of them. But the spaghetti still kept swelling up and soon all four saucepans were overflowing.

"Oh dear, oh dear, oh dear," cried the queen and she ran and fetched four more saucepans. She put some spaghetti into each of them.

But still the spaghetti kept swelling up and soon all
eight saucepans were overflowing.

"Oh dear, oh dear, oh dear, oh dear," wailed Queen
Nellie. "I haven't got any more saucepans!"

Luckily, by then the
spaghetti was cooked.

Queen Nellie looked round her kitchen. Spaghetti had wriggled out of the saucepans and slid down the cooker. Spaghetti had slithered and wiggled across the kitchen floor; coils and twirls of spaghetti, twists and curls of spaghetti, everywhere spaghetti!

"Would you believe it," said the queen. "I think I've cooked too much. Much too much."

She knew the King would be upset. If there was one thing King Jim disliked, it was waste.

So Queen Nellie gave some of the spaghetti to her cat Binks to eat.

"Come off it, Queen Nel, Ma'am," said Binks as he tried to eat it. "Cats like fish, not string. Even a nice mouse would go down better than this lot."

He ate a saucerful just to please the queen but there was still an awful lot left.

Then the queen called her dog Barker and gave him some of the spaghetti to eat.

"Dogs like meat, Your Maj," said Barker as he tried it. "Not hot wet worms. Even a nice bone that's been buried in the garden for a few months would go down better than this lot."
He ate a bowlful just to please the queen but there was still an awful lot left.

So the queen called the royal peacock Strutter and gave him some of the spaghetti to eat.
"Peacocks like tasty insects, dear Highness," said Strutter with a shudder. "Not heaps of squiggly-wigglies. Even a few dry spiders would go down better than this lot."

He picked at a few strands just to please the queen but there was still an awful lot left.

The queen looked at the clock. As quickly as she could she stuffed most of the spaghetti back into the pans. Then she hurried to the back door, carried the pans outside and emptied them on the grass. She called her hens and ducks.

"Eat!" she commanded in her most regal voice.

The hens and ducks were rather surprised. They had already had their dinner and were getting ready for bed.

"What can it be?" quacked the ducks.

"Let's try it and see," cackled the hens.

So the hens and the ducks pecked and pulled and tugged and scratched at the spaghetti.

Spaghetti wound round their legs,

spaghetti tied up their beaks;

sticky ropes of spaghetti,
clingy strings of spaghetti,
everywhere spaghetti.

"Hurry up!" shouted Queen Nellie from the kitchen window. "Get that mess cleared up!"

So the hens and ducks clucked and snacked and gulped and quacked until they were so full of spaghetti they could hardly move.

But there was still an awful lot of spaghetti left.

Then Queen Nellie noticed her geese slap-dashing up the path to see what was going on.

"Just in time," she said. "Come and finish this up!"

So the geese hissed and squabbled and honked and gobbled until they were so full they could hardly move. But there was still an awful lot of spaghetti left.

Queen Nellie felt desperate. Then she
had a brain wave. She rushed down to
the royal pigsty and let out all the pigs.
The pigs were delighted.

They wallowed and puffed,
and swallowed and stuffed,
and tucked in and sucked in
delicious spaghetti as fast as they could;
they grunted and snorted
and squealed and cavorted,
they slurped and they burped
and they...

...ATE IT ALL UP!

"What a delicious smell," said King Jim as he hung up his hat and put on his indoor crown. "Spaghetti for supper," he continued, washing his hands. "My favourite, and your spaghetti is always so good, my dear. Yes, I worked so hard making money all day that I am very hungry tonight."

Queen Nellie passed the spaghetti round, adding some of the tasty tomato sauce and a sprinkling of grated cheese on top.

The spaghetti was good. The sauce was scrumptious.

"I hope there is plenty more," said King Jim, passing his plate over. "I'm still quite hungry."

But there wasn't any. There wasn't
a scrap of spaghetti left anywhere!

For Isabel

First published by HarperCollins in 1991
This paperback edition published in 2015
Text © Patricia Cleveland-Peck 1991/2015
Illustrations © Tim Archbold 1991
Cover design by Anna Lubecka

1 3 5 7 9 10 8 6 4 2

ISBN 978-0-00-811875-4

HarperCollins is a division of HarperCollins Publishers Ltd

Visit our website at: harpercollins.co.uk

Printed and bound in China